The hall was suddenly filled up with noisy kids rushing to class.

Hundreds of legs seemed to be everywhere. Salem tried to run in between the legs walking by, but it was too confusing. He was spinning in all directions.

"Salem!"

Salem heard Sabrina call, but he couldn't do anything about it.

"Whoa!" The legs seemed to carry him away. As he was spun around, he passed rooms filled with desks, saw students at lockers—and sometimes he even saw the ceiling.

Then the bell sounded again. The hundreds of legs vanished, leaving Salem all alone in a hallway. He looked around. "Help! Sabrina!" he shouted. "Is anyone out there?"

No one responded, and Sabrina was nowhere in sight. "This is just great," he said to himself. "Now who's going to wait on me?"

Sabrina, the Teenage Witch™
Salem's Tails™

#1 CAT TV
#2 Teacher's Pet

Available from MINSTREL Books

Sabrina the Teenage Witch

Salem's Tails™

TEACHER'S PET

Patricia BARNES-SVARNEY

Illustrated by Mark Dubowski

A MINSTREL® BOOK

Published by POCKET BOOKS

New York   London   Toronto   Sydney   Tokyo   Singapore

This book is a work of fiction. Names, characters, places and incidents are products of the author's imagination or are used fictitiously. Any resemblance to actual events or locales or persons living or dead is entirely coincidental.

A MINSTREL PAPERBACK *Original*

 A Minstrel Book published by
POCKET BOOKS, a division of Simon & Schuster Inc.
1230 Avenue of the Americas, New York, NY 10020

Sabrina, The Teenage Witch: Salem's Tails
Based on Characters Appearing in Archie Comics
And the Television Series Created by Nell Scovell
Developed for Television by Jonathan Schmock

Salem Quotes taken from the following episodes:
Pilot episode—Teleplay by Nell Scovell
Television Story by Barney Cohen & Kathryn Wallack
"Mars Attracts" written by Nell Scovell
"A River of Candy Corn Runs Through It" written by Frank Conniff

ISBN: 0-671-02381-0

First Minstrel Books printing November 1998

10 9 8 7 6 5 4 3 2 1

A MINSTREL PAPERBACK and colophon are registered trademarks of Simon & Schuster Inc.

SABRINA THE TEENAGE WITCH and all related titles, logos and characters are trademarks of Archie Comics Publications, Inc.

Cover photo by Pat Hill Studio

Printed in the U.S.A.

To Paula Berinstein, cat-lover . . . and good friend . . .

"Oh, right, I forgot. I'm an animal. I have no self-control."

—*Salem*

Chapter 1

"Yi—ouch!" Salem yelled as two books from the bookshelf crashed down on him.

"Salem, do you mind?" Sabrina Spellman said, lifting some papers on her desk. "I'm trying to find something."

The black American shorthair cat looked up at Sabrina and tilted his nose into the air. "Well, so am I," he said, looking around the room. "But how can you tell where anything is in this room?"

Sabrina frowned at her talking cat. "Believe me, Salem. I know where everything is in this room."

Salem sniffed and turned back to the

bookshelf. "Then where is that book *Cats, Cats, and Cats?*"

"Got me. Maybe Aunt Zelda sold it at her witch's garage sale. Remember? When she was trying to raise money for a new magic vacuum . . . I think." She scratched her head. "Or was it for the Witches' Council?"

Salem scowled. "Stop. You're giving me a hairball."

"The Witches' Council isn't that bad," she said.

"Ha! So how do you explain Drell?" Salem snorted.

Sabrina bit her lower lip and shrugged. "Bad subject."

Salem was not just any black cat. He could talk.

After all, Salem had been a warlock at one time. He tried to take over the world, but he failed. Drell, the head of the Witches' Council, punished Salem Saberhagen by turning him into a black house cat for a hundred years.

Right now he was living with the teenage Sabrina Spellman and her two aunts, Zelda and Hilda. They were all witches. Well, Sabrina was half witch and half mortal, but that was all right with Salem. In fact, he thought all the Spellmans were all right—for witches without fur.

"I *would* have to live in the only house in Westbridge without the right cat book," Salem grumbled. He had been looking for the book for a day now, and he was sure it must be around here somewhere. Who would throw such a book away? After all, he just *knew* it would give some details about the cats he'd seen in the neighborhood. And there was no doubt it would point out that American shorthair cats were the best and smartest in the world. *And that's information I can really use—*

3

to get some respect around here, he thought.

"Why are you so interested in finding the cat book?" asked Sabrina.

"Just curious."

"Really?" she said, raising an eyebrow.

Salem knew that tone of voice—and he knew he couldn't keep the real reason from Sabrina. "Oh, well," said the cat, sighing. "If you must know, I want to find out . . . I mean, *confirm* that American shorthair cats are better than all the other cats."

"And?"

"And which cats were worshipped in ancient Egypt," he said, swatting a book aside with his paw. "Or how other cultures have treated cats. Face it, cats have kept humans in line for centuries."

"Been there. Heard that. And?"

"You sure are nosy," he said. He stopped his search, curled up on Sabrina's desk, and wiped a whisker. "All right. I saw a great show about cats on the Animal Channel last night. If I can prove to everyone how perfect and wonderful cats are—"

"Get it out of your head," warned Sabrina. "The Spellman family will not worship you—cat or not."

Salem licked his left paw. He suddenly stopped, remembering he was not really a cat. "Not even a *little*?"

"No," Sabrina said firmly. "I don't have time to argue about your greatness. I have to get ready for school. Not only do I have a history test, but I'm having a hard time with a math problem in Mrs. Quick's algebra class."

"Is that why you slept late?"

Sabrina glared at him. Turning, she pointed a finger at her desk. The papers flew into two neat stacks. "No. I was up late studying for the history test and my

5

witch's test, too—so I was tired. It's hard to do both schoolwork and witch work."

Salem looked at two of Sabrina's books. "At least you don't have to carry around *The Discovery of Magic* book," he said.

Sabrina was studying to get her witch's license. She carried her *Magic Handbook* around the way her friends carried around their *Driver's Handbook*. The other magic book, *The Discovery of Magic,* was given to Sabrina on her sixteenth birthday by her father—the day her aunts told her she was a witch. It was leather, studded with many jewels on the front, and much too bulky to stuff in her backpack. "Yeah, I'd need a wheelbarrow to carry it around," she answered.

Salem snickered. "I don't see why you have to go to school." He hopped up on the bed. "I don't have to learn things in a school. I just know things. Go ahead. Ask me anything."

"All right," said Sabrina, putting her hands on her hips. "When did the Spanish-American War begin?"

Salem stared at her. "I don't remember any Spanish-American War. What are they teaching you at that school?"

Sabrina shook her head. "Wrong answer, Salem. There *was* a Spanish-American War," she said.

"Oh, I really don't have time for this," he said. He jumped down from the desk. "Now, where is that book?"

Sabrina rolled her eyes. "Right. Now it's time for you to . . . uh-oh! Speaking of time, what time is it?" she said, turning to a clock on a nearby table. "Oh, great—clear the way!" she yelled, grabbing a towel and running to the shower.

Salem shrugged as he watched Sabrina run out the door. Turning to the bookcase, he carefully crawled up the shelves. Pulling

himself onto the top shelf, he grabbed a book.

"Nope. Wrong one," he said, then tossed the book over his shoulder to the floor. As he reached for another book, two more books tumbled off the shelf. Salem winced as the first book smacked a doll on the second shelf and the other book hit a box of paper clips, scattering them all over the floor.

"Uh-oh! I'd better get out of here." Salem jumped, knocking over three more books in the process. He slipped on a thick, black book and tumbled upside down—right into Sabrina's open backpack sitting on the floor.

"Help!" he cried. "Cat overboard!"

Salem tried to get out of the backpack. He yanked and pulled, but he was stuck. Turning his head, he saw the problem: A sticky tab on the inside of the pack had caught the fur on his back.

He struggled again, trying to spin around to reach the tab. Every time he moved, the gummy tab pulled on his fur.

"Ouch! Ouch!" he yelled. He pushed away one of Sabrina's hairclips. "Yuck. Hello! Is anyone out there?"

No one replied. Salem drummed his claws on a nearby book. "Great. Now I have to wait for Sabrina and her hour-long shower. I don't see why she spends so much time in the . . . wait a minute." Salem tried to snap his fingers. Then he remembered he had paws.

"Maybe it isn't so bad in here after all," he whispered to himself. "I could go to school with Sabrina. Maybe I could prove to her that school isn't as hard as she thinks. Maybe they have some great books on cats. Maybe in the library. Maybe some of the students truly appreciate cats there! Lots of maybes in there, but it's worth a try."

Salem was very proud of himself and his idea. He snuggled down into the backpack and pulled a few of Sabrina's notebooks over him.

"Westbridge High School, here I come!" he said, closing his eyes.

Chapter 2

I feel like I'm on a ship during a big, bad storm, thought Salem. He'd been in the backpack for about a half hour—and Sabrina still had no idea he was there.

Reminds me of the time I told Christopher Columbus to sail west for a new trade route. Poor guy, if this is how he felt . . .

It was crowded in the sack. Sabrina had stuffed some papers on top of him as she hurried to pack for school.

Even though he tried to push things out of the way, he could hardly move. He tried to move his back left paw, but it was pinned under Sabrina's history book. He

11

tried to move his back right paw, but it hit an old bag of potato chips. If the bookbag shifted right, Sabrina's spiral notebook poked him in the ribs. And the tabs were pulling on his thick fur.

How much longer? Salem thought, rocking back and forth. From the noise outside, it sounded as if they were close to school. But Salem still couldn't tell.

The black cat sighed. He reached over and pulled out a round case. Opening it up, he almost sneezed.

"Ahhhh . . . ahhh . . ." he started to say. Quickly putting a paw to his nose, he stopped the sneeze. "That was close," he whispered to himself. He looked closely at the round case again.

No wonder. He read the outside of the case. *"Angel Skin face powder." Eeewww.*

Salem felt as if he had been in the pack for weeks. To pass the time, he hummed softly to himself. He pretended that he was the King of Cats, being carried around by his person. He also had a good time tearing up a white tissue he found, and he chewed on a piece of paper that was tickling his nose.

But it wasn't *all* fun in the backpack. Sabrina wasn't very gentle. After all, she didn't know that Salem was inside. She was walking fast to school because she was late, so sometimes she would jog, bouncing Salem up and down. Then she would switch the pack from one shoulder to the other.

I'm starting to get seasick—

Salem suddenly heard sounds of school. Students were talking all around him and he heard lockers opening and closing.

"Hey, Val! Over here!" Salem heard Sabrina yell. He knew Valerie was one of Sabrina's good friends.

"So, have you seen Harvey today?" Val asked Sabrina.

13

Salem chuckled.

"What was that?" he heard Sabrina say. He covered his mouth with his paw. "I thought I heard someone laugh. Anyway, no. I think Harvey's going to the dentist this morning. Sounds like he gets out of the history test for now."

"Gross. I think I'd rather take a history test," answered Val.

Sabrina suddenly dropped the pack on the ground.

"Oof!" Salem said softly. The history book moved, pinning down his tail. Gritting his sharp teeth, he tried not to yell.

At this point he almost changed his mind. He wanted to yell at Sabrina to let him out, but he really wanted to go to school. The possibility of reading new books and proving Sabrina wrong was just too tempting.

Salem felt Sabrina pick up the pack again. She tossed it over one shoulder, causing Salem to flip on his side. He tried to sit up, but it was no use. Panting, he gave up and laid his head on a notebook.

I bet the ancient Egyptians never treated their cats like this, he thought. *Then again, I don't think they had backpacks.*

Salem heard Sabrina spin the lock on her locker. The door opened with a *clang!* and she threw the backpack inside the locker.

"Ouch! Now, this is going too far!" Salem muttered. He was caught between a notebook and the potato chip bag.

Suddenly something poked him hard in the ribs—and this time it wasn't a book. It poked him again, and Salem stayed quiet.

"Uh, Val," Salem heard Sabrina say. "I'll see you in class. Okay?"

"Was it something I said? Wait, I only said I didn't like the dentist, so you can't be mad at me for—"

15

"Val!"

"All right. But hurry," came Val's answer. "You know Mr. Watson likes us to be on time for tests. What am I saying—*I* like to be on time for tests."

Salem heard Val's footsteps fade down the hall. Then he was poked again as the top of the backpack flew open.

"Ah-ha!" Sabrina said, grabbing Salem by the scruff of the neck. He felt one of the tabs pull at his fur.

"Hey, watch the merchandise!" Salem cried.

His head popped out of the backpack and he looked at Sabrina. "Tell me. Do all teenage girls carry this much junk in their backpacks?" he asked calmly. "Pens. Papers. Notes. CD player. Notebooks. Books. Makeup. Wrinkled potato chip bags. A stick of gum that looks as old as I am—"

"Salem!" Sabrina made a growling sound in her throat. She glanced around the hallway. No one heard her yell—they were all busy walking to class or talking.

"What are you doing here?" Sabrina whispered, pushing him farther into the locker and blocking his view of the hall.

"*Moi?*" he asked. He tried to act as if he did this every day.

"Yes, you!" Sabrina took a deep breath. "What are you doing here?"

"Would you believe I wanted to help you at school?" he whispered.

"No."

"All right. How about I was looking for a pen?"

"No."

"Ummm . . . I was looking for a lost can of tuna and knew you kept everything in your backpack?"

Sabrina started to answer but suddenly stopped.

"Hi, Sabrina," said a voice behind her. "I just made it back from the dentist."

17

"Oh, Harvey. Hi! Great!" Sabrina said, stuffing Salem all the way to the back of the locker.

"Ouch!" Salem wiggled away from her hand. He poked his head above the backpack. "You'll ruin my fur," he whispered.

Sabrina glared at him and pushed his head back down. Her face quickly changed into a smile as she turned back to Harvey. "See you in class? I just have a few notes to grab."

"You sure you don't want me to wait?"

"No, that's okay . . . thanks," Sabrina said.

Salem tried to say something, but she pushed his head down again.

"Mmmfphit . . ."

"Okay. Sure. See you there," came Harvey's reply. Salem heard Harvey walk away.

Sabrina turned to Salem, squinting her eyes. "Don't say it, Salem."

"What? That your boyfriend looks better as a frog?"

Sabrina frowned. "Listen. Let me use my magic and pop you back—" she said, raising her finger to point to Salem.

"No! Wait!" he whispered frantically. "I don't want to go home. Not just yet."

"Then I'll stuff you in my locker."

"No way," he answered, stamping a paw. "Cats don't like to be stuffed. Maybe with food, but—"

"Salem, you can't stay here. I mean, it's like having one of my aunts follow me around school."

"I am not one of your aunts," he said, tilting his nose into the air. "Now, listen. Didn't you want to show me that school was hard?"

"Well, yes. But you usually ignore me and my requests," she said, folding her arms.

"Not this time. I'm all ears. We'll make

19

a deal. You don't interfere with my school day, and I don't interfere with yours. No zapping me—at all. Okay?"

Sabrina looked around the hallway, then at her watch. "Oh, all right. You and I will go to school today. I really don't have time to argue—I have a history test in three minutes." She did not wait for a reply. She grabbed the backpack, complete with Salem inside. "Here's the deal the way *I* see it— I won't use a spell on you at all today. And as for you: No scratching. No hairballs. No talking to humans . . . and stay put if I say stay put," she added, slamming her locker.

Salem rocked back and forth in the backpack as Sabrina hurried to class. "Like I have a choice," he said, sighing.

Chapter 3

Salem was developing a bad case of boredom.

He sat in the backpack as Sabrina took her history test. He batted around a pen and drummed his claws on a notebook. Then he tried to brush his fur with Sabrina's hairbrush. To kill some more time he tore up another white tissue.

It was just too boring. He couldn't take it anymore!

Salem popped his head out of the backpack and looked around the room. "My, my. A room filled with lemmings, all taking the same test," he muttered under his breath.

Sabrina looked down at her pack on the floor, then pushed Salem's head back down.

"Hey!" Salem muttered. "It's crowded in here. You're bending my whiskers!"

Sabrina leaned down, putting her face near Salem's. "That's not all I'll bend," she whispered. "Now, get back in—"

"Miss Spellman?" said Mr. Watson. The history teacher looked up from his desk at the front of the class. "What's the meaning of this?"

Sabrina gulped.

Salem gulped, too.

"Ummm. His name is Salem, sir," said Sabrina, picking up the cat.

"Tell him I'm here to explain the true history of the world to his class," Salem muttered under his breath to Sabrina.

Sabrina put her hand over his mouth. "He must have fallen asleep in my pack, Mr. Watson. I promise he'll be good."

"I was *not* asleep. I was just resting," Salem mumbled behind Sabrina's hand.

Mr. Watson rubbed his chin. "All right. He's been quiet so far. You can keep him here. But don't let him bother the other students. You all have a test to take."

Sabrina nodded. Salem jumped out of Sabrina's arms, landing on her desk. "Just be quiet," she hissed. She picked up a pencil and went back to the test.

Salem peered over Sabrina's pencil. "I don't see why you have to take tests anyway," he whispered. "Just use your magic. How about a spell?"

Sabrina scowled at him.

Salem looked at the test paper. His eyes opened wide. "Napoléon?" he whispered just a little too loud. "What does that paper say? He knew nothing about taking over the world! Now, Alexander the Great, he was really something. That's why they called him 'great'!"

23

Sabrina glanced up and noticed two students were staring at her. "Uh . . . sorry. I get upset sometimes. History makes so many wild claims. Alexander the Great was really great, you know . . . I think."

The two students tried to smile. Then they turned back to their tests.

Sabrina glared at the cat. She pushed her long blond hair over her shoulder, and turned back to the paper.

The cat lay down on the desk. If he tilted his head just right, he could read Sabrina's test. "Uh-oh," he blurted out in a whisper. "Sure, Alexander Graham Bell invented the telephone. But did you know he was great at hide-and-seek, too?"

"Do you mind, Sabrina?" said the girl across from Sabrina. "We don't really care about your problems with history."

"Uh, right." Sabrina tried to smile, but it looked more like a grimace. She pushed Salem off the desk. The black cat landed on all four paws. Then he lifted his nose and snorted.

Sabrina sighed and turned back to her test.

"I bet other kids would appreciate my help," he mumbled to himself.

Salem wandered around the room. Two boys and three girls patted him on the head. One girl even scowled at him, and Salem scowled back. But most of the students were busy taking the test.

He was getting bored again. No one was paying attention to him.

He sighed and wandered back toward Sabrina. As he walked by a girl with long black hair and big blue eyes, she reached down. He smiled as the girl rubbed him behind the ears.

Oh, yes, I can never reach back there, he thought as he quietly purred.

Sabrina coughed, trying to get Salem's

25

attention, but he ignored her. He liked the cute girl who was paying attention to him.

A bell suddenly rang and Salem jumped. Sabrina dropped her test on the teacher's desk, then scooped Salem up in her arms. "Time to go," she said.

"Hey, I wasn't finished," he whispered.

Sabrina dropped him into her pack. "I am," she said, lowering her voice. "That was Jessica Steele. She's a new girl at school. I don't know anything about her."

"Awww . . . are you jealous?" Salem asked, batting his eyes.

"Don't be silly," she said. "I just don't know what she's like."

"Cute, if you ask me," he said, sighing. "She said I was the cutest cat she's ever seen. She can feed me grapes any day."

"Oh, brother," Sabrina said. "You don't even like grapes!"

Sabrina walked quickly down the hall to her locker.

Salem popped up and looked over her shoulder. "Sixty-six. Forty-four. Twenty-two."

Sabrina stopped turning her lock. "Salem, what are you doing?" she whispered.

"Saying some numbers. Maybe one will be a magical number—and your locker will open. By the way, why don't you just use your magic to open this thing?"

"That's not the point. And stop saying numbers—you're confusing me." She turned back to the lock.

"Hey, Sabrina," said a blond-haired boy. He opened the locker next to Sabrina's locker. "Neat cat."

"Hi, Max," answered Sabrina. "Thanks."

"Here, guy," said Max. He pulled a long, yellow string out of his pocket and held it out to Salem. "Come on. Grab this. Here ya go."

Salem tilted his head, staring at the string as it danced up and down. As the string came close to Salem's face, the cat slashed at it with his paw—coming close to Max's hand.

"Hey!" Max yelled, pulling back his hand.

Sabrina turned so Salem faced away from Max. "My cat doesn't really like to play, Max. You know. Allergic to string."

Max shrugged. He put the string back in his pocket, then leaned toward Sabrina. "All cats like to play with string. Yours is probably just tired."

"Tell him we also like to put spells on humans," Salem whispered in Sabrina's ear.

Sabrina poked her backpack. "Gotcha. I'll remember that. Thanks, Max. See ya," Sabrina said to the boy. She watched Max turn and walk away.

"If I could do just one spell," Salem said quietly, "he'd be a rabbit right now. A rabbit with big ears. A rabbit with big ears and a big nose." He plopped his head down on Sabrina's shoulder.

"Now, calm down, Salem," Sabrina whispered. "We have other things to think about right now. Like what am I going to do with you?"

"You can scratch me behind the ears," he answered. He wiggled the rest of the way out of the backpack and jumped in Sabrina's locker.

"No way," Sabrina whispered. "Why don't you let me send you home? All it takes is the point of a finger," she whispered, holding up her hand.

"Nope. We had a deal. No spells."

"But you know, you look really, really bored. Why don't you just walk home?"

"Nope again. I like it here," he insisted. He held up his left paw. "Plus, I have delicate paws. Anyway, you're supposed to show me why school is so hard. And why it's so great."

29

"Oh, be that way." She grabbed the cat, pushing him into her backpack again. Then she closed her locker.

Salem pouted as he swayed back and forth in the backpack. It did not seem fair. He wanted Sabrina to prove that school was hard, but she just seemed to be mad at him. He was trying to be good, and he really wasn't causing *that* much trouble. What was wrong with a cat going to school anyway?

It seemed like centuries before Sabrina stopped. When she set her pack down, Salem stuck his head out and stared at the gibberish on the blackboard.

"Is she speaking English?" he whispered to Sabrina, nodding to the teacher at the blackboard.

"Shhhhh." Sabrina held a finger up to her lips. She pointed to her algebra textbook.

"Yuck." Salem shook his head. "Any

math that requires more claws than I have is math I'll never need again."

Sabrina pointed a threatening finger at him.

"Hey, you promised. Okay, okay. I get the point. Time for my eleven o'clock nap anyway."

Salem snuggled back into the pack and fell asleep.

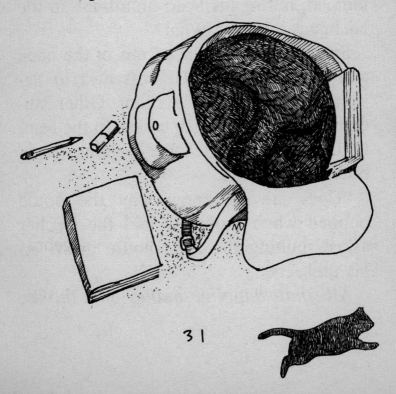

Chapter 4

op!

Something cracked near Salem's ear. He jumped, hitting his head on a book in the backpack. "What? What?"

Salem popped his head out of the pack and looked around. He was next to Sabrina at the back of a room. Other students sat around six lab tables. In the front of the class stood a teacher, holding a soda bottle in his hand.

"Does anyone know why the bottle popped when I opened it?" the teacher asked, putting the soda bottle down on his desk.

All that napping makes me thirsty,

thought Salem, licking his lips and looking at the soda bottle. *Skip the soda—I could use a big bowl of milk right now.*

Sabrina raised her hand. "Mr. Snyder, is that the same experiment that's on page forty-four in our science book?"

The substitute science teacher blinked. "Someone actually read the book?"

"Yes, and it looks like the same experiment. There's pressure in the bottle. It's caused by carbon dioxide gas. So when you open up the bottle . . . *Poof!* It pops."

"That's right," Mr. Snyder answered. "The gas expands, causing the bottle to make a popping noise when it's opened. Carbon dioxide is very good to us. And very good, Sabrina."

Salem hopped up on Sabrina's lap and smiled. "Way to go," he whispered.

Sabrina put a hand over Salem's mouth. It was too late.

Luckily, Mr. Snyder didn't hear Salem

whispering. He did see the black cat move, though. "And what do we have here?"

Salem froze.

"Umm. He's . . . Well . . ." Sabrina picked Salem up in her arms. "This . . . this is Salem, Mr. Snyder. My cat."

Salem turned to Sabrina. "I'm not your cat. You're my person," he muttered under his breath.

Sabrina frowned at the cat, then she turned back to Mr. Snyder. "He fell asleep in my backpack. And I didn't have time to take him back home. He won't be any problem. Really."

Mr. Snyder reached down and patted Salem on the head. "Just don't get near the mice," he said to Salem. He pointed to the mouse cage in the corner. Three white mice were in the large cage. One mouse chewed on a piece of cardboard. Another one was asleep on an old sock, while the third one drank water from a bottle.

Salem shivered.

"He doesn't like mice, Mr. Snyder. In fact, he faints at the sight of mice. Right, Salem?" Sabrina said.

Salem made a growling sound in his voice. "Me-ow," he said, looking up at the teacher.

"Oh, all right. I guess he can't cause that much trouble," answered Mr. Snyder.

Sabrina smiled and put Salem on her desk. "Now, stay."

"Not even a please?" Salem whispered.

Sabrina glared at the cat. Salem rolled his eyes at Sabrina and sat down.

"All right, class. Back to work," said Mr. Snyder. He stopped and looked back at Salem. "You know, we *could* talk about science and cats today."

Salem looked at Sabrina and shook his head. "Me? A science experiment? I am a cat, *not* a guinea pig!" he whispered, panicking.

"Uh . . . I don't really think—" Sabrina started to say.

"We can show how the cat's tongue is rough and scratchy. We can see that they don't have round eye pupils like humans, but slits. And maybe we can see how his paws and claws look. How about it, Sabrina?"

Salem didn't hear what Sabrina said. Everyone started talking and cheering at once.

The teacher smiled and headed toward Salem. As he reached the cat, Salem dashed between his legs. He ran toward the front row of lab tables.

Salem jumped up on the front desk, knocking over the soda bottle. He was still really thirsty, but the sticky liquid didn't look appetizing. As he tried to run across the desk, the soda coated his paws—and his paws stuck to several papers. *Oh, this is just great*, he thought, *stuck on science.*

"Here, Salem," someone said. Salem looked up and noticed that Mr. Snyder was heading his way.

Salem scurried off the front desk and jumped up to the top of a nearby bookshelf.

The teacher walked up to the bookshelf. "Come on, Salem. I won't hurt you."

The cat blinked. "Cowabunga!" he whispered to himself—and jumped to the top of the mouse cage.

The mice ran in all directions. Salem put his face to the glass cage and smiled. One mouse hid under the cardboard, and the two other mice tried to hide under the old sock.

Salem brought out his claws. Just as he was about to swat the top of the mouse cage, Sabrina appeared at his side.

"Oh, no, you don't. Not this time," she

said, scooping up the cat in her arms. Sabrina walked quickly back to her seat and set Salem into her pack. Then she plopped down into her seat and ignored Salem. "I don't think he likes the attention, Mr. Snyder," she announced. "Can we just use the book instead?"

Salem tilted his nose in the air. "Gee, Sabrina. I was just trying an experiment of my own."

Salem was so tired he slept through the next class. It was time for his sixth nap of the day—and he had had only three so far. *Time to catch up,* he thought as he fell asleep.

Not only that, he could tell that Sabrina was really, really mad at him. She wasn't talking to him—and she wouldn't even look at him.

He felt Sabrina grab the pack. *We must be heading for the next class,* he thought.

As he snuggled into the pack, he saw a light. Sabrina was opening the backpack.

"Now what?" He yawned—and smelled something wonderful.

"Be quiet and stay out of sight," Sabrina whispered. "You'll really be in trouble if they find you here. I mean it, Salem. Stay put."

Salem peeked over the top of the pack. He was under a table in a big room—and he smelled food. *This isn't a class, it's the cafeteria!* he thought, looking around. *I know I'm going to like this place.*

"I'll go get us something to eat. You stay here." Salem watched as Sabrina headed for the food line. He knew he was very hungry. After all, his stomach was growling.

Salem smacked his lips as Sabrina brought a tray with two sandwiches, potato chips, and a bowl of mushy yellow stuff back to the table. "Let's hurry up and eat before Val and Harvey get here. I don't want you making a scene."

"Can I have some of that?" Salem asked, ignoring Sabrina and pointing to a sandwich. He was much too hungry to chatter. "And what's that?" He pointed a paw at the yellow stuff.

"It's vanilla pudding," she said, giving him tuna from the sandwich and some pudding. He quickly gobbled down the food.

"Ahhh," he said, smacking his lips several more times. Then he licked his pudding-sticky paws. "That was good. I'll have to order that yellow stuff at home."

"Order?" Sabrina frowned. "Don't get carried away, mister."

Sabrina finished her sandwich and piled the used plates on the tray. She gently pushed Salem's head into the pack. Putting the pack over her shoulder, she headed for the tray disposal.

Salem peered over the top of the pack and noticed they were getting close to a huge bowl of vanilla pudding sitting on a nearby counter.

It was too much for Salem. He looked both ways and smacked his lips. No one was watching—so he jumped, almost on top of the pudding bowl!

A woman behind the counter screamed. Salem screamed, too, then ran out the door.

Bam! The cafeteria door slammed shut.

Salem's tail just missed getting caught in the closing door. He was running at full speed, but it was hard to run on the tile floor. "Why can't they carpet the school halls?" he said as his claws kept slipping.

"Salem! Wait!"

It was Sabrina.

Salem tried to stop—but his feet didn't stop. It felt as if he were on a sheet of ice!

Sabrina caught up with Salem and

scooped him up. "Salem! I told you to stay with me."

"It was a choice between you and the vanilla pudding," he mumbled. "But I guess the pudding was unable to fulfill its duty as a winner. So now you win."

Sabrina sighed and put Salem into her pack. "Oh, come on. Classes are changing soon."

She walked to her locker and grabbed a book and a notebook. "I don't know why I ever made this deal with you. You're just getting into too much trouble."

"Hey, give a cat a chance!" Salem jumped down from the backpack and stood in Sabrina's locker. He really wanted to see what was so special about school. As he stood there, he listened to several students talking about a science fair. Two other students were talking about a concert.

"So what's so hard about school?" he

asked under his breath, standing close to Sabrina. "It seems simple. You take a few tests. You nap. You go to class. You nap. You eat lunch. You nap."

Sabrina bent down toward Salem. "I guess you weren't paying attention," she whispered. "It's not that simple. And *I* didn't nap in any of my classes." She reached into her locker, trying to pull out something from the back.

Suddenly two students rushed by. Sabrina was pushed off balance, almost falling. The book she was pulling out nudged Salem out of the locker and onto the floor just as the bell for class rang. The hall was suddenly filled up with noisy kids rushing to class.

"Uh-oh!" A foot just missed Salem.

Hundreds of legs seemed to be everywhere. Salem tried to run in between the legs walking by, but it was too confusing. He was spinning in all directions. Some students reached down and petted him. Others laughed as he became tangled in the group.

"Salem!"

Salem heard Sabrina call, but he couldn't do anything about it.

"Whoa!" The legs seemed to carry him away. As he was spun around, he passed rooms filled with desks, saw students at lockers—and sometimes he even saw the ceiling.

Then the bell sounded again. The hundreds of legs vanished, leaving Salem all alone in a hallway. He looked around. "Help! Sabrina!" he shouted. "Is anyone out there?"

No one responded, and Sabrina was nowhere in sight. "This is just great," he said to himself. "Now who's going to wait on me?"

Chapter 5

Salem felt his heart sink.

He had been walking up and down the hall for almost a half hour, hiding whenever he heard footsteps. When he peeked, it was never Sabrina. "She *would* have to get lost," he muttered. "And she probably won't use magic to find me after the trouble she had with Roland the Troll and his finder spell." Sabrina had used Roland to help find her notebook and ended up locked in a castle, about to be married to the troll until Harvey saved her.

Not only that, Salem was still thirsty. All he saw were closed doors and lockers. Then he saw what he was looking for: a water fountain!

He stared up at the tall fountain. "It's made for humans, not cats," he growled. "I may start a new law. Lower water fountains for cats. It's only fair. Cats get thirsty, too."

Salem looked both ways and noticed no one was coming. He put his front paws on the wall and stretched as tall as possible. He was still too short to reach the fountain. "Oh, well. I guess I have to jump. Heard of leaping lizards? This is leaping cats."

He backed down the hall and stopped. "One. Two. *Three!*" Salem ran as fast as he could, leaping into the air—and just catching the edge of the water foundation. His left paw slipped, his claws scrabbling at the porcelain. But he grabbed the side again and pulled himself up.

"Whew!" he said, panting. "Now. Let's see. How does this work? What happens if I push this?" Salem pushed a button—

and a stream of water splashed him in the face.

He sputtered, then wiped the water off his face with a paw. He pushed the button again. *Splat!* He was smacked in the face with more water.

"I want a drink, not a bath." Salem said, sighing.

He jumped down to the floor and wandered down the empty hallway, reading the signs on the closed doors. Suddenly he stopped.

"The library! Finally! Maybe Sabrina will be in there."

Salem eyed the door, then reached a paw up toward the door handle. "Now . . . if . . . I . . . can . . . just . . ." He sighed as he missed the handle. "Why is everything up so high? It would be so much easier if I were human. Or a dog. Did I say that? I must be delirious."

Salem knew he couldn't open the door.

He looked at a trash can across the hall, noticing that there was just enough room for him to hide out of sight. He snuggled into the corner—and waited.

Soon a young boy went into the library. Salem leaped from the corner, just sneaking through the opening as the door swung shut.

Salem laughed quietly to himself, noticing that the boy didn't realize Salem was there. *Chalk one up for the super-stealth cat.*

Salem knew he had to hide again, so he ran from chair to chair. At one point he peeked over a chair, looking for Sabrina. He saw a woman with pointed glasses standing behind a counter. There were also some students studying at tables and others searching for books on the shelves. But he didn't see Sabrina.

Salem stopped behind a stack of books sitting on a table. Putting his paws on the table, he looked around. *So far, so good*, he thought, *no one has seen me.*

He looked up at the stack of books. Tilting his head, he read the top book on the stack. "There it is! *Cats, Cats, and Cats!*" he whispered happily, leaping up on the table. "I've been looking for this—"

"Eeeeeeek!"

Salem turned his head and rolled his eyes. "Now what?" he whispered. After all, this was a library. Who would be making such a racket?

The lady with the glasses was pointing at him. "A cat! It's a cat! Get the cat!"

Salem looked around. "Where? Where?" he said. Then he shook his head. "Uh-oh, she means me!"

Students started running in all directions. As someone shouted in his ear, Salem hopped from the table, knocking over the stack of books.

"See if I ever come to *this* library again,"

he huffed. As he ran for the library door, two girls were walking out. This was his chance to escape!

Salem made a mad dash for the opening. He jumped into the hall, right past the two girls.

"I made it!" He turned left down the hall—and realized he made a wrong turn.

Standing there was a janitor with a mop in his hands. He didn't look friendly.

Salem turned and raced the other way. He ran down a hallway to the right and hid behind a bushy potted plant.

The janitor was getting closer to Salem. "Here, kitty, kitty, kitty," said the man.

Salem growled and popped up. "Kitty?" he muttered under his breath. "I am *not* a kitty." He walked out from behind the plant. "I am a powerful warlock."

The janitor smiled at Salem. "Good kitty," he said. "Come here, kitty, kitty." The man reached out for Salem. "Gotcha!"

Salem ducked—and the janitor slid across the floor.

The black cat scooted down the hall, not looking back.

Sabrina was right—and how often do I say that? Salem thought, running as fast as he could. *School is hard!*

Chapter 6

That's it. I'm going home," Salem announced to himself. "Now all I have to do is find a door."

Salem was hiding behind an open classroom door. Classes were changing, and he didn't want to get caught. Once in a while, he'd peeked out, hoping to see Sabrina walk by. It was no use—Sabrina was nowhere around. *That's it*, he thought, *I'm certainly not going to keep looking for her. I have naps to take.*

As the bell rang and the last student went to class, Salem sighed. He was tired of waiting for Sabrina, and he was sore from running away from people. More than anything, though, he was getting hungry again. *I sure wish I could jump into a huge bowl of vanilla pudding*, he thought, smacking his lips. *Maybe I should just look for the cafeteria door and call it a day.*

Instead, he strolled out from behind the door and headed down the hall, searching for a way to get outside. Soon Salem came face-to-face with a large brown door under a bright red sign that read EXIT. He smiled and pushed.

The big door didn't budge. He wasn't heavy enough to push it open, and he couldn't reach the door's metal bar. But there was hope. The door was slightly open, and he could smell fresh air from the outside. If only he could squirm out by pushing through the thin opening.

Salem pushed the door with his nose, then with his paws. The door didn't budge—and he still couldn't fit through the opening. "I guess I shouldn't have had that extra helping of pudding," he said, patting his stomach with his paw.

Salem heard the wind pick up outside. As he watched, the wind swirled around, slowly inching the door open. "Just . . . a . . . little . . . more . . ."

The wind caught the door, opening it wide. Salem jumped through the opening just before the door slammed shut.

"I'm free!" he shouted. "Oh, yuck."

Salem looked around and shivered. He was finally outside—but he was also standing in a drenching rainstorm.

He took a deep breath and let it out slowly. "Maybe this wasn't such a good idea after all. I don't know the way home. And me without my Crispy Crumbly Crunchy Cereal compass."

He decided not to wander too far from the school. Sabrina might be looking for

him, especially when classes got out.
"Then again, when do classes get out?" he
said. "Now look. I'm talking to myself. Oh,
well, what better person to talk to?"

He shivered again. "Good thing I was a
witch scout," he said. "No problem here.
I'm prepared. I'll make a fire to stay warm.
All I have to do is find two sticks and rub
them together."

Salem streaked over to the cover of a
tree. He nosed two small sticks closer together, but he couldn't hold them with his
paws. "Hmmm. I think this worked better
when I was young. And human."

Something hit him on the head. Looking
down, he saw an acorn. Looking up, he
saw a squirrel on a branch above him.
"What are you? Nuts?"

The squirrel ignored him and dropped
another nut on Salem's head.

"Hey, watch it! I hope no one sees this,"

Salem said, panting and ducking. "A princely cat being chased away by a nutty squirrel!"

Salem ran through a parking lot and across an open field of grass. Then he turned right down an alley between two buildings. Running by a broken fence, he ducked under it.

Then he looked around and gulped.

Westbridge High School was nowhere in sight.

Salem ran back toward the alley. Everything looked different from what he remembered. "I could have sworn I took a right here," he said, scratching his head. It started to rain harder, and he ran back to stand under the broken fence. As he watched the rain fall, he sat down and sighed. "I certainly can't stay here all day."

Suddenly something caught his eye. At

the end of the street was a phone booth. "That's it! I can call Hilda and Zelda! I'll tell them what happened to me—and they'll pick me up here. Wherever 'here' is . . ."

Stopping on the wet sidewalk, he looked up—and realized that he had a problem. " 'Local calls, thirty-five cents,' " he read on the phone. "Thirty-five cents?" He looked down at his paws. "Hey, what about us cats? We don't come with pockets. Or money."

It just wasn't Salem's day. He continued down the sidewalk, his paws squishing as he walked. He stopped and looked across the street, eyeing several people standing on the sidewalk. "A bus stop!" he yelled.

Coming up the street was a big bus. *Well,* he thought, *even if it isn't going in the right direction, if I stay on long*

enough, it's bound to go past the Spellmans' house. Eventually. I think.

He ran across the street and stood quietly with the other people. No one seemed to pay much attention to him.

Salem waited patiently as the bus came to a stop. He watched as two women and a man entered the bus. But when he tried to hop up the stairs, he saw a boot coming in his direction.

"Scat, cat!" the bus driver yelled. The bus driver was booting him off the bus!

Salem stepped back as the bus door slammed shut, his ears flattening against his head. " 'Scat, cat'? Did you say, 'Scat, cat'? I'll have you know that I was once—"

The bus roared away as Salem held a paw in the air. "I'll turn you into a goat! I'll turn you into a lizard! I'll—"

A car drove by. It hit a puddle of water, soaking Salem.

He sputtered. "And you, too!" he yelled
at the car.

Salem walked down the sidewalk. He
was dripping wet and miserable—and trying to remember when he had ever had
such a terrible day.

Chapter 7

All Salem really wanted was to be home. "I should have let Sabrina use a spell to send me home," he said. "I'd do anything to be playing with the television remote right now. I'd even let Sabrina watch her favorite show. But just this once."

He shook his head, spraying water everywhere. He looked up and saw a woman carrying an umbrella and a large sack to a car.

"All right!" he whispered to himself.

This time he'd be smart.

This time he'd sneak into the car. *Then* he would tell the woman what he wanted.

He raced up to the car and hid behind the front tire. As the woman opened the back car door, he slipped inside. "Great. A taxi cab," he said, sniffing as he settled in the backseat. "Ready when you are," he said, turning to the startled woman. "To the high school, my good woman."

The good woman's eyes went wide. She tried to take a breath.

Then he remembered. "Uh-oh," he whispered. He should not be talking to a mortal. They really didn't understand talking cats.

Uh-oh, he thought, wincing. *Here comes the screaming part—*

The woman looked at Salem and screamed. She dropped her umbrella and sack and ran into a nearby garage.

"No, wait a minute! I can explain—" Salem jumped into the front seat, putting his paws on the dashboard. The woman grabbed something and headed back to the car.

She had a broom in her hand.

"Wow. Cool broom. Is she a witch?" he said.

The woman walked to the car door, swinging the broom toward Salem. "Shoo, cat!"

Salem ducked. He tried to jump into the driver's seat. But the woman was too quick with the broom.

"Shoo!" she yelled again. "Get out!"

Salem ducked again, trying to jump out of the car. He finally slipped past her, dropping to the sidewalk.

"And I didn't even get to ask her if I could borrow the umbrella," he muttered, running down the rain-soaked street.

Salem was still outside, getting water-logged in the rainstorm.

He felt as if he had been wandering for

days. He was almost ready to give up when he saw a big redbrick building in front of him.

It was Sabrina's school!

He didn't know the time, though. Was school out already? Was Sabrina gone? "I think I'm going to invent a cat watch," he said. He knew it was late. It just *had* to be the end of the school day.

Salem walked around the school, trying to find an open door, but he was out of luck. All the doors were closed.

"Ah-choo!" Salem sniffled. "I never knew school was so hard. It's hard to get *out* of school. It's hard to get *into* school. . . ."

He looked up and stopped. There was just what he needed—an open window. "Well, if I can't get into the school through a door . . . Hmmm . . . maybe it is good to be a cat sometimes."

Salem jumped, his front paws landing on the windowsill. But he wasn't there for long. The sill was slippery from the rain, and he had just enough time to peek in the open window—before he slipped off.

He grimaced as his claws scrapped down the side of the wall. "This is not the right way to sharpen my claws," he said, slowly sinking down.

Salem sat in a heap on the ground, feeling even more cold, wet, tired, hungry—and cranky. He heard someone laughing in the distance. "Oh, be quiet," he muttered, scowling even more.

Suddenly he shook his head. If someone was laughing, the person probably had to come out through an open door. Maybe that door was still open.

Salem jumped up and ran toward the laughter. As he turned around a corner of the school, he saw a group of kids. They were talking just inside the school's front doors, hiding from the rain.

Sabrina was one of them!

Yippee!

Salem felt wonderful. Finally he could go home! Finally he could get out of the rain! But when he started to yell to Sabrina, he stopped.

"Wait a minute. If Sabrina sees that I'm wet, she'll start to ask questions. Then I'll have to admit that I, the great Salem, got lost," he said. He shook his head and stood up straighter. "No way. *I* don't get lost. *She* gets lost. But I'm still not saying anything right now."

Salem ducked behind a nearby tree. He looked up, expecting to see the nasty squirrel, but the branches were empty. "All the really smart animals are out of the rain," he whispered, sighing.

Staying close to the wall of the building, he slowly sneaked toward the school entrance. Carefully he ran up the side of the stoop and slipped inside the school's propped-open door. No one noticed him—

they were all too busy talking and laughing.

Salem saw several backpacks on the ground. There, sitting in the middle, was Sabrina's open backpack. He waited until the students were all laughing again. Then he raced for the backpack, jumped in, and landed on a notebook. Pushing with his nose, he poked under the notebook to hide. He was ready for the bumpy ride home.

The black cat fell asleep. After all, he'd missed several naps today. Once in a while he would feel the bounce of the backpack, or he would hear people talking. But he was very tired. All he wanted to do was snuggle down and snore away the rest of the afternoon.

Plop!

Salem woke up with a start. The backpack was on the ground.

He yawned and stretched. This time he'd fool Sabrina and act like a cat.

The top of the backpack opened. "Ah, meow, meow, meow!" he said, squinting from the sudden light.

No one said anything back.

No one told him to stop fooling around.

Uh-oh.

Salem's eyes blinked open. Sabrina was nowhere in sight.

Salem gulped. "Meow?" he said, looking up at the person in front of him.

There was Jessica Steele, the cute girl from Sabrina's history class.

Chapter 8

"Oh, kitty!"

"Meow?" Salem tried again.

Jessica smiled at Salem. She put her hand out to the cat and scratched him under his chin. Despite his worry, he stared to purr again.

"I know who you are," she said, still scratching him. "You're Sabrina's cat, Salem. Boy, was she ever worried about you."

Salem tilted his head. He could not believe it. Sabrina was really worried about him? He felt a little warmer knowing that Sabrina was really concerned.

"Now, let's see," Jessica said. She pulled

Salem out of her pack and carried him to a linen closet. Opening the door, she pulled out a bright red towel. "There," she said, wrapping Salem in the towel. "You should be warmer now."

Jessica carried Salem back to her backpack, then put him down on the floor. As she searched through her backpack, she frowned.

"Just look at this," she said, holding up a wet notebook.

"O . . . Meow," he said, correcting himself. He batted his eyes for effect.

"I can tell you're sorry," she said, shaking out the notebook. "Don't worry. It'll dry out. I just hope you will, too."

Salem curled up in the towel. He watched as Jessica stood up and walked over to a phone. She pulled out a telephone book and dialed.

"Hello?" she said. "Sabrina?"

Salem lifted his head. "This ought to be good," he whispered.

"Sabrina," Jessica was saying into the phone. "This is Jessica Steele. I'm in your history class. . . . Yeah, that's me. I think I have something that belongs to you. . . . No, it's bigger than a notebook. . . . It's black . . ."

"It?" mumbled Salem, scowling.

"And it has claws . . . and it was very wet when I took him out of my backpack," she said, laughing.

"Oh, great," he whispered, putting a paw on his forehead. "Now I'll never hear the end of this."

"Sure," Jessica continued. "He's meowing up a storm. Almost like he wants to tell me something. . . . Yeah . . . Don't you wish cats could talk? . . . Okay, see you soon. Bye."

Jessica hung up the phone and walked over to Salem. "Your Sabrina is coming,

Salem," she said, looking into Salem's eyes. "Sabrina says she's glad cats can't talk. I wonder why?"

Salem thought he was dreaming.

Jessica was paying a great deal of attention to him. She fed him tuna fish in a big bowl, but it was not the usual tuna fish from the Spellman house. This was special tuna in springwater. He was so hungry, it took only a minute for him to gobble it down.

After he ate, Jessica brought out a light blue brush. "It looks as if you've been out in the rain for a while," she said. "Your fur is a mess. Will you let me brush you?"

Salem rolled his eyes and moved closer to Jessica. As she began to brush his back, he started to purr again.

"Ooohhh!"

"That's weird," she said, looking closer at his back. "It looks as if you have a chunk of acorn caught in here. I wonder how that happened?"

Salem shivered, remembering the nasty squirrel. Then he purred again, wondering how long it would take to train the Spellman women to give him brushings.

A half hour later Salem heard the doorbell ring. But he was too busy to pay attention. Jessica was sitting on the floor, doing her homework, while Salem was lapping up milk from a bowl.

"That's your owner, Salem," Jessica said, standing up and walking to the front door.

"Owner? Owner?" he sputtered. "If anything, I own her. She just so happens to be *my* person."

Sabrina walked into the living room. If he could, Salem would have folded his arms. Instead, he turned his back to Sabrina and lapped up the rest of his milk.

Sabrina glared at him. "Yes, that's Salem,

all right," she said, turning to Jessica. "Thanks for calling me."

"No problem," Jessica said, reaching over and picking up Salem. "He's really a wonderful cat."

Salem put his nose in the air. *At least someone appreciates me.*

"Uh, yeah, wonderful," said Sabrina, holding out her hands to Salem. "Come here, wonderful cat." Only *she* didn't sound like she meant it.

Salem backed away, snuggling closer to Jessica.

Jessica looked surprised. "I don't know why he's like this," she said. "All I did was give him tuna and some milk."

Sabrina smiled. "Oh, he's probably just a little cranky because he got lost at school. You know how cats are." Salem squirmed again, glaring at Sabrina.

Jessica's mother peeked in from the kitchen. "Jessica, I don't mean to interrupt. But would you help me unload the dryer? It'll only take a minute."

"Okay, Mom," she said. She handed a struggling Salem to Sabrina. "Be right back."

Sabrina waited until Jessica walked through the kitchen door. Then she turned to Salem, holding him up until they were nose to nose.

"Before you say anything, Sabrina," he said, holding up his paw, "I want you to know—I'm not going back!"

Chapter 9

"Look here, Salem—"

"*You* look here, Sabrina," Salem interrupted. He tried to make a fist with his paw, then gave up. "You think I'm a *little* cranky? First, you make this dumb deal with me about no spells—"

"*You're* the one who wanted—"

"Then you get lost at school—" he continued.

"*Me*? You were the one who wandered away!"

"Then," he said, ignoring her, "I get stuck out in the rain with no change to make a phone call—"

"What change? Where would you keep it—"

"That's not the point. . . . Now, where was I . . . Oh, yeah, and here," he said, holding his paw out, "they treat me like the King of Cats!"

"In other words, they wait on you hand and foot . . . I mean paw and paw?"

"Cute. I bet Jessica would let me choose the television programs I want to see. She would brush my fur. She would feed me vanilla pudding. She would—"

"Never understand how it's possible that you can talk," Sabrina added.

Salem stopped. He looked up at Sabrina. "Well . . ."

"So how could you even tell her you want vanilla pudding? She'd go running out the door screaming the minute you asked," said Sabrina. "It would be only milk and canned tuna forever."

Salem gulped.

"But I guess you really want to stay here," she said. "I'm sure we will cope somehow. Oh, and you can forget about the book of magic. Or the linen closet. And no more Drell."

Salem perked up. "No Drell?" he asked. Not seeing the head of the Witches' Council would be a good thing.

"But what if Drell said you didn't have to be a cat anymore?" said Sabrina. "How would we get hold of you?"

Salem was silent. Then he sniffed. "No magic book?" He loved to relive his days as a powerful warlock by pawing through Sabrina's book of magic.

Sabrina shook her head.

Salem sniffed again. "No linen closet?" The Spellman linen closet was a portal to the magical Other Realm, where Salem could freely mix among other witches.

Sabrina shook her head again.

He sniffed once more. "And no vanilla pudding?"

"Nope," Sabrina answered.

"Well, I guess I can't let the Spellmans down. I can see you all need me." He jumped out of her arms and padded to the door. "Do ask the school for their vanilla pudding recipe, will you?"

Sabrina rolled her eyes and shook her head as Salem walked out the front door.

Salem was finally home. As he and Sabrina reached the Spellman's front door, he stopped. "You know, I've been thinking about your school. I think I'm really going to miss it in some ways."

"Really?" Sabrina asked. "You mean you've changed your mind about school? Do you think it's fun? That's it's not so easy?"

Salem scratched his head with a paw. "Hmmm. Well, I guess I agree with you now. It is hard."

Sabrina laughed and clapped her hands together. "Yes! You're finally saying that I'm right about something!"

"In a way," he said. "Yes, school *is* hard. It's really hard to remember your locker number. I'm bad at numbers. I'm better at remembering spells." He sat down on the porch. "And it's hard to look for a library book when someone is chasing you—"

"Salem, you know that's not what I mean!" said Sabrina, scowling at the cat.

"And it's hard to find people. And, boy, was it hard trying not to talk to mortals," he said, ignoring Sabrina and continuing with his list. "Oh, and walking on the slippery floors. Wow. *That* was tough. And—"

Sabrina opened the front door and walked into the house. "What's the use. I'll never convince you." She sighed deeply.

"Oh, all right," he said, following her inside. "Maybe it *is* a little hard. But I could teach you a few more things about history if you let me."

"Yeah, the *wrong* things," Sabrina answered. "I'll take my chances with the schoolbooks, thank you very much. Aunt Zelda! Aunt Hilda! We're home!"

"In here!" came a call from the kitchen. Sabrina picked up Salem and pushed open the kitchen door.

Standing there were Zelda and Hilda, both dressed in bright, flashy costumes. The kitchen was decorated with crepe paper and balloons. And standing next to Sabrina's two aunts was a real donkey.

"Surprise!" Sabrina, Zelda, and Hilda yelled.

"What's this all about? And what's that donkey doing in the kitchen?" asked Salem, his eyes going wide.

"It's a welcome back Salem party!" said Zelda. "You know. Cake. Crepe paper. Favors. Balloons. Candles. Witch's brew."

"And pin the tail on the donkey!" added Hilda, holding up a pin.

"Just to let you know we missed you,

Salem," said Zelda, trying to push the donkey out of the way.

"Here," said Hilda, handing Sabrina a donkey tail. "It's your turn to pin the tail on the . . . well, I guess he already has a tail. Never mind."

"Which reminds me—speaking of animals," said Sabrina, pointing her finger. A book appeared in her hands. "I found this book on cats in the library. Isn't this the one you wanted, Salem?"

Salem looked at the cover. It was *Cats, Cats, and Cats!*, the book he was looking for all this time! As Sabrina set the book in front of him, he smiled. "Oh. You *do* care."

Sabrina grinned. "Maybe. But just a little. Don't get a swelled head."

Salem opened the book and skimmed the text. As Sabrina and her aunts started to cut the cake, Salem whistled. "Hey, wait, guys! It says right here that American shorthair cats' high intelligence develops as we grow. That means I was right—we're all super smart!"

"Yeah, but from what I hear, not smart enough to come in out of the rain," said Hilda.

"Ouch. That hurts." He turned to the book again. "Now, let's see. 'American shorthair cats,'" he read, "'are typically always with people.' True. But it has to be the right kind of people."

He looked around the Spellman kitchen and sighed happily. All was right with Salem's world again.

And you know what? thought Salem. *The Spellmans are the right kind of people.*

Cat Care Tips

#1 Cats should always have fresh food available, since they like to eat frequently throughout the day and night. Cats should eat a good, well-known brand of cat food, since they have very specific nutritional needs. It is fine for them to have snacks of human food if you want to indulge them, but their main diet should always be cat food.

#2 Make sure the cat food you use says that it is completely nutritionally balanced for cats. Try to vary the flavors that your cat receives (unless you have specific instructions from your veterinarian). Cats should not have tuna fish flavor too often.

#3 Never, never let your cat go on a food fast— if he or she does not eat the type of food that you are giving within twenty-four hours you must try another flavor or type of food. Cats will not eat food that they do not like, no matter how hungry they get, and they can get very sick if they don't eat for as few as three days. Cats **do not** follow the rule that when they get hungry enough they will eat whatever food you have selected.

—Laura E. Smiley, MS, DVM, Dipl. ACVIM
Gwynedd Veterinary Hospital

About the Author

When she's not playing in the catnip with her favorite cat, Artie, the author is usually writing nonfiction science and science-fiction books and articles. Her books include *Sabrina, The Teenage Witch: Magic Handbook* as well as several from *The Secret World of Alex Mack* series and the *Star Trek: Starfleet Academy* series for young readers. Her hobbies include hiking, herb gardening, rock hunting, and birding. She lives in Endwell, New York, with her husband. She also tends to sundry squirrels, chipmunks, birds—and cats, including, of course, Artie.